Dear Hunter —
We bought this book while we were vacationing
in Hawaiʻi — It is a good story, and we hope you
enjoy learning some Hawaiian words —

Tūtū and the ʻUlu Tree

We love you — Gma Marilyn & Gpa Wayne
Christensen   7-6-2013

For my many mo‘opuna
and
all the children of Hawai‘i

ISBN 1–56647–043–9

For information on other MnM books contact:
Native Books
P.O. Box 37095
Honolulu, Hawai‘i 96837
(808) 845-8949
Fax (808) 847-6637
Printed in Korea.

Tūtū and the ʻUlu Tree

Created and written by
SANDRA L. GOFORTH

Illustrated by
Christine Joy Pratt

Pillow designed by
Betty Rose Rezentes

The city faded as the car rounded the sweeping curve and the Wai'anae coast came into view. The children knew it wouldn't be long before they got to Tūtū's house.

Tradewinds rustled through the many trees surrounding Tūtū's house. Early this morning, she gathered and strung plumeria blossoms to make *lei* (flower garlands) for her *moʻopuna* (grandchildren), Chad and Chelsea. While she waited, she worked at her quilt frame.

Jumping from the car,
the children shouted,
"Tūtū! Tūtū!"
With *lei* on her arm,
she called, "Come give me
a big hug."

The *keiki* (children) raced to the house. "Don't forget. Take off your slippers." Tūtū laughed.

On the porch, Chelsea pointed to the quilt. "That's pretty, Tūtū."

"*Mahalo* (thank you). I've been working on it for a long time."

"Chad, come look at Tūtū's quilt."

"That's girl's stuff."

"'*A'ole* (no), Chad. Some of the best quilts are made by men," Tūtū explained. "Your Uncle Akamu cut this design when he wasn't much older than you."

Chad chased a gecko across the porch. "What's it supposed to be? It looks like a snowflake."

"What else does it look like?" Tūtū asked.

"A flower?" Chelsea suggested.

"That's close."

"It looks kinda like a pineapple."

Tūtū shook her head.

"A grenade!" Chad said.

Tūtū smiled, "*kolohe* (rascal), you know better than that."

"It's an *'ulu*. That's Hawaiian for breadfruit.
Have you ever heard of breadfruit?" Tūtū asked.
Both children shook their heads.
"How can fruit be bread?" Chad asked.
"A fruitcake, silly," Chelsea joked.
"I'll show you. Let's go to Aunty Betty's."

Chelsea was surprised. "We have another aunty?"

"Kind of. She's your *hānai* (adopted) aunty."

"Hā. . . nai?" Chad said.

"She's my best friend. In Hawai'i we have big families. Friends are family, too."

Aunty Betty looked up from her weeding when Tūtū and the *keiki* arrived. "What a nice surprise. I thought you'd be quilting this early in the morning."

"My *mo'opuna* came for the day. The children have never seen *'ulu.*"

A magnificent tree stood in the center of the backyard. Its branches sagged beneath the weight of the round, bumpy, warty-skinned fruit.

Chad pointed to the *'ulu*. "It looks like your quilt."

"Is it good to eat?" Chelesa asked.

"*'Ae* (yes). *'Ulu* is *'ono* (tasty). The *'ulu* is a very special tree. It is important to our way of life. It represents growth and life to Hawaiian people. There's an old Hawaiian proverb, *'ka 'ai nānā i luna'* which means *'ulu* is a food that requires looking up to." Tūtū said.

Chelsea reached up, "The leaves are so big."

"Some leaves grow to be as long as your arm. The tree grows very tall, too." Aunty Betty explained.

"As tall as a giraffe?" Chelsea asked

Tutu pointed to the tree top. "Maybe as tall as two giraffes."

"Why don't we have a little picnic?" Aunty Betty asked. "We'll eat and talk story."

"Where'd *'ulu* come from?" asked Chad.

"A long time ago early Polynesians brought *'ulu* cuttings to Hawai'i. *'Ulu* grows better from cuttings than from seeds, and *'ulu* was one plant they didn't want to leave behind," Tūtū answered.

"Why?" Chelsea asked.

"Because they could make many things from the *'ulu* tree." Aunty Betty replied.

"*'Ulu* was as important as *kalo* (taro) because one tree produces enough fruit to feed a family for a year. Polynesians made *poi 'ulu* (pounded *'ulu* paste). We can make *pepeie'e 'ulu* (breadfruit pudding) and fried *'ulu* chips. Maybe we'll have some for lunch." Tūtū said. "Why don't you tell them about the Bounty."

"Have you heard about a ship called the HMS Bounty and its visit to Hawai'i? You know, Captain Bligh and Fletcher Christian?" Aunty Betty asked.

The children nodded.

"The Bounty came to collect *'ulu* cuttings and take them to the British West Indies. Landowners there thought *'ulu* would be a perfect food for their workers. The Bounty was a floating *'ulu* garden."

Chad picked up a small pebble and threw it against the tree. Overhead chattering mynah birds abruptly took flight.

"That reminds me," Tūtū said. "Long ago, there were *kia manu* (bird catchers). They caught and plucked feathers from the *'i'iwi* and *'ō'ō* birds to make feather capes and *lei*."

"How'd they catch the birds?" Chelsea wanted to know.

Aunty Betty made a small cut in the *'ulu* tree bark. A milky, sticky gum oozed out. "With this," she answered. "It's called *kēpau*."

Chelsea touched it. "It's sticky."

"After spreading *kēpau* on the branches, they whistled bird calls. The birds landed on the sticky branches. Because it was hard for the birds to fly away, other *kia manu* hiding in the bushes had enough time to snare the birds. Then they collected a few feathers from each bird. When they were *pau* (finished), they set the birds free to let them grow more feathers." Aunty Betty explained.

"Sort of like recycling, huh?" Chad said.

Tūtū laughed, "You could say that. *Ka po'e kahiko* (the ancient ones) used every part of the *'ulu* tree. From the trunk's light wood, they made *papa he'e nalu* (surfboards), *papa ku'i 'ai* (poi pounding boards), and *pahu* (drums), and special parts for their canoes. They even used *kēpau* on canoe seams to keep the water out."

Aunty Betty added, "*keiki* liked to chew on the tree stems. *Ka poʻe kahiko* used the leaves for medicine and the milky sap as a salve for cuts and scratches. The Hawaiians polished their calabashes, *kukui* nuts and other things with dried *malo ʻulu* (ʻulu leaf covering)."

Spreading her arms wide, Tūtū said, "And, the *pua'a* (pigs) got so big from eating the scraps and peelings."

Aunty Betty cut an *'ulu* fruit and some leaves from the tree. "Be careful when you handle *'ulu*, because the sap will stain your hands and clothes. Here, take these home with you. Tūtū can make you some pudding."

"Will you, Tūtū? Please, please." Chelsea begged.

"Of course. Do you want to come, sister? I think I could use some help."

After a lunch of fresh fish patties, rice, *'ulu* chips, and *pepeie'e 'ulu*, Tūtū showed the children how to cut an 'ulu pattern snowflake stlye.

"Keep in mind what the *'ulu* looks like, then draw your design."

"If you want, you can trace around the leaves," Aunty Betty added.

The children worked hard tracing their leaves and drawing the fruit.

"Now, you're ready to cut." When they were finished, she said, "Let's see what your 'ulu pattern looks like." Slowly, they opened the paper patterns. Each was different.

"It's beautiful," exclaimed Chelsea.

"Yeah. That's pretty neat," added Chad.

Holding up one of the lacy designs, Tūtū said, "This pattern could be used on a pillow or as a quilt square. When we make big quilts, we just make the designs larger. Remember, to make good patterns, you must first understand the plant."

"Do you think Uncle Akamu would like mine?" Chad asked.

" '*Ae*. He would. He'd be proud of you both," Tūtū said.

After Aunty Betty left, the children watched as Tūtū began to quilt. She smiled while she stitched. "That will be a happy quilt," Chelsea said.

"Why do you say that?"

"Because you look happy when you sew it," Chelsea answered.

"*Mahalo* (thank you). You're right, my dear. When it's *pau*, my *mana* (spirit/soul) will be in the quilt."

"*Mana*?" Chad quizzed.

"*'Ae, mana*, my spirit, a touch of my soul. I want to fill the quilt with my happiness so whomever receives it will always feel my presence. Hawaiian quilts are special because they hold the quiltmaker's *mana*."

It was nearly dark when the children's mother came. The children gathered up their paper patterns, their *'ulu* leaves and fruit. Tūtū kissed and hugged everyone.

"See you next week," they called as they climbed into the car.

Tūtū smiled, " *'Ae*, my sweet *mo'opuna*, until next week."

— *Pau* —

Glossary

'ae   yes

'a'ole   no

ali'i   royalty

hānai   adopted, either legally or spiritually

'i'iwi   hawaiian bird prized for its red feathers

ka 'ai nānā i luna   food that requires looking up to

kēpau   gum or resin, as on ripe breadfruit

luana iki   pause a moment to enjoy yourself

kalo   taro plant

ka po'e kahiko   ancient Hawaiians, the people of old

keiki   children

kia manu   bird catcher

kolohe   rascal, sassy

lei   necklaces or garlands of plants or flowers

mahalo   thank you

maika'i   very good

malo 'ulu   dried leaf covering used like sandpaper

mana   spiritual, divine power, presence, essence

mo'opuna   grandchildren

'ono   tasty

'ō'ō   hawaiian bird valued for its
   yellow feathers

pahu   drums

papa he'e nalu   surfboards

papa ku'i 'ai   poi pounding
   boards

pau   finished, completed, all done

pepeie'e 'ulu   breadfruit pudding

poi   cooked, pounded taro or breadfruit

'ulu   breadfruit

Wai'anae   a town on the leeward coast of O'ahu

Let's Eat

NOTE: This activity should never be undertaken without adult supervision. Children should only be allowed to assist in preparation of food and not permitted to do any cooking, baking, or frying.

PEPEIE'E 'ULU (Breadfruit Pudding)

3-4 cups ripe breadfruit
1-1/2 tsp. salt
1 cup Sugar
1-1/2 cups coconut milk
3 tsp. cinnamon, optional

Preheat oven to 350. Scrape ripened pulp from breadfruit. Add salt, sugar, milk and cinnamon. Pour into buttered dish. Bake for 1 hour.

'ULU CHIPS

1 -2 green breadfruit
oil for deep frying
salt, to taste

Using green breadfruit, peel (with a vegetable peeler), quarter and slice. Soak in ice water for one hour. Dry thoroughly between dish towels (wet slices will cause hot oil to splatter). Deep fry in hot oil until slightly brown and crisp. Fry only a few at a time. Do not crowd fryer. Drain on paper towels and salt while still warm. Store in air-tight container.

Let's Cut Snowflakes

NOTE: This activity requires adult supervision.

SUPPLIES NEEDED:

Large pieces of freezer or butcher paper
Large pieces of colored construction paper
Glue or paste
Scissors
Pencil

INSTRUCTIONS:

1. Cut colored construction paper to make a square.

2. Fold colored construction paper into eighths, fold in half, then in half again, and finally into a triangular half.

3. Draw free hand a breadfruit leaf or trace a leaf. If tracing, be sure to place only one-half of the leaf on the fold. (To get an exact one-half fold, cut along the leaf mid-rib.

4. Cut design.

5. Open and glue it to larger piece of paper. This can be used as a bookcover or framed and given as a gift.

Kēpau Picnic Ant Trap

NOTE: This activity requires adult supervison.

SUPPLIES NEEDED:

Styrofoam trays (You may recycle by using washed meat trays or
  bento boxes)
Kēpau (*'ulu* tree sap)
Sugar
Knife
Spatula

INSTRUCTIONS:

1. Make several diagonal cuts in *'ulu* stem.

2. Collect *kēpau* with spatula.

3. Smear the *kēpau* on bottom of trays.

4. Sprinkle very lightly with sugar.

5. Place traps on the four corners of picnic table. The sugar will
   attract the ants and the *kēpau* will trap them.

Instructions for Making Pillow Top or Quilt Square

SUPPLIES NEEDED:

Background fabric — cut one 16" square
Applique or top fabric — cut one 16" square
  (traditionally black material is not used)
Batting (3 oz. is preferable) — cut one 16" square
Lining fabric (may be lightweight fabric) — cut one 16" square
Pillow back fabric — cut one 16" square
Thread to match applique material
Quilting thread
Needles (#7 In-Betweens quilting needle, applique needle)
Sturdy hoop or square plastic pipe frame

INSTRUCTIONS:

1. Trace pattern from page 37 and cut out tracing.

2. Folding Fabric: (instructions for folding apply to both background fabric and applique fabric) Fold both pieces of fabric separately as follows.

   a. Fold material in half and press.

   b. Fold material in half once again (it is now folded into quarters) and press.

   c. Take one corner and fold to the opposite corner to form a triangle and press.

(i) The long side is called the bias.

(ii) The short side is called the straight.

3. Place the pattern on the folded applique material and either staple it or pin it securely, making sure that you match the bias to bias edge and straight to straight edge. Carefully cut out the pattern.

4. Open folded background material and note folded press lines. Unfold cut applique and place on top of background material, pinning centers together. Carefully spread applique design so as not to stretch the fabric on the bias. Diagonal lines should be placed on diagonal press lines and straight lines on straight press lines. Continue to pin around the design. Baste the applique design to the background material about 1/2" from the raw edge.

5. Applique with small blind stitches (overcast stitch), turning the raw edge under. For inside curves, make several increasingly smaller stitches to prevent fraying. When applique work is complete, lay out lining square and place batting square on top. Place the appliqued design on top of the batting. Securely pin all layers (like a three layered sandwich) and baste together to form a 3" grid pattern.

6. Quilting: Stretch the appliqued block in hoop or square, stretching taut. The quilting stitch is done in small straight up and down even stitches (be careful not to do a "running stitch" - quilting stitches are achieved by piercing the fabrics with a straight down stitch [perpendicular] and returning with a straight up [perpendic-

ular] stitch. Begin by quilting directly around the edge of applique design ("in the ditch"). Then return to the applique design and quilt the interior, bearing in mind the markings on the fruit, flower or stem. If you do not know how, simply do an echo pattern of the shape. When you have completed the center, you then proceed to add rows of "echo" quilting following the shape of the design, spacing your rows approximately 5/8" apart.

7. You may frame your project, make it into a pillow, or make several blocks and join them together as a quilt. It is suggested that if you desire to make several blocks for a quilt, you do not quilt them individually, but rather join only the applique squares together and then quilt the entire project. If you choose to make a pillow, complete with either cording or matching bias binding; this pattern square will accommodate a 14" pillow form.

LUANA IKI (Pause a moment to enjoy oneself)

Illustration of Pillow Pattern

Bias

Straight edge

Pattern for 15"pillow
Trace to make template

See page 34 for instructions

NOTE: The same folding and cutting techniques can be applied when using paper. Children will enjoy cutting a design and pasting it to another piece of paper to make a picture or book cover.

Bibilography

Abbott, Isabella Aiona. *La'au Hawai'i: Traditional Hawaiian Uses of Plants*, Honolulu: Bishop Museum Press, 1992.

Belknap, Jodi Parry. *Majesty, The Exceptional Trees of Hawaii*, Honolulu: Outdoor Circle.

Dunford, Betty. *The Hawaiians of Old*, Rev. ed., Honolulu: Bess Press, 1987.

Fitzsimmons, Lorraine F. *Hawaii for Today's Children*, Rev. ed., Honolulu: University of Hawaii, 1966.

Hawaiian Designing Quarterly. — 2nd Issue, 1982

Lamb, Samuel H. *Native Trees & Shrubs of the Hawaiian Islands*, Santa Fe, NM: Sunstone Press, 1981.

Lucas, Lois. *Plants of Old Hawaii*, Honolulu: Bess Press, 1982.

Moon, Jan. *Living With Nature in Hawaii*, 3rd ed., Hilo, Hawaii: Petroglyph Press, 1987.

Nordhoff, Charles. *The Bounty Trilogy*, Boston, MA: Little, Brown, 1951.

Pukui, Mary Kawena. *New Pocket Hawaiian Dictionary*, Honolulu: University of Hawaii Press, 1992.

Schwenke, Reginald L. *Grandma Lily, Polynesian Cultural Center's Hawaiian Quilter*, Honolulu: Gus Hanneman, 1984.

Scott, Susan. *Plants and Animals of Hawaii*, Honolulu: Bess Press, 1991.

Tuell, Bonnie. *Island Cooking, Favorite Hawaiian Islands Recipes*, Wailuku, Maui: Maui Electric.